Also by Heather Grovet

Ready to Ride Series
A Perfect Star
Zippitty Do Dah
Good As Gold
More titles coming!

Other books by Heather Grovet
Beanie: The Horse That Wasn't a Horse
Marvelous Mark and His No-good Dog
Petunia, the Ugly Pug
Prince: The Persnickety Pony That Didn't Like Grown-ups
Prince Prances Again
Sarah Lee and a Mule Named Maybe
What's Wrong With Rusty?

BLONDIE'S BIG RIDE

Heather Grovet *Series Book Four*

READY TO RIDE SERIES

Pacific Press® Publishing Association
Nampa, Idaho
Oshawa, Ontario, Canada
www.pacificpress.com

Book design by Gerald Lee Monks
Cover illustration © Mary Bausman

Additional copies of this book are available by calling
toll-free 1-800-765-6955 or by
visiting http://www.adventistbookcenter.com

Library of Congress Cataloging-in-Publication Data

Grovet, Heather, 1963-
Blondie's big ride / Heather Grovet.
p. cm. — (Ready to ride; bk. 4)
Summary: Ten-year-olds Megan, Kendra, and Ruth-Ann and
their ponies join the Cancer Trail Ride to raise money for
Cancer research to help their riding instructor, a young woman
who has been diagnosed with breast cancer. Includes safety rules
for horse riding.
ISBN-13: 978-0-8163-2225-1 (pbk.)
ISBN-10: 0-8163-2225-2
[1. Ponies. 2. Breast cancer. 3. Friendship.
4. Christian life. 5. Canada.] I. Title.

PZ7.G931825Bl 2008
dc22
2007026044

08 09 10 11 12 · 5 4 3 2 1

Dedication

To my husband, Doug, who helps with fencing, hauling bales, and mucking stalls, even though he isn't a real horse person!

Contents

Riding Lesson News

It was a scorching summer morning, and ten-year-old Megan Lewis felt hot enough to melt as she trotted her Palomino pony, Blondie, around the riding ring. Megan's friends, Kendra Rawling and Ruth-Ann Chow, were also riding their ponies during today's lesson, and Megan suspected both girls were as hot and tired as she was.

"OK, everyone!" called Trish, the riding instructor. "Good job! But we need to rest so your ponies don't pass out in this heat."

The girls halted in the center of the arena and grinned at each other. Recently the three girls had formed a club called Ready to Ride

(R2R). Now they spent their time together taking lessons, trail riding, and just enjoying everything about their ponies.

Trish Klein, their instructor, wasn't actually part of their club, but she had been a direct answer to prayer. Trish loved God, kids, and horses, so she was the perfect teacher for the girls!

Megan was riding Blondie, the middle-sized pony of the three. Her real name was Good as Gold Blondie. The little mare was half Morgan and half Welsh. Blondie was slightly chubby but beautiful with her golden coat and thick blond mane and tail that matched Megan's own blond hair.

Beside Megan sat Kendra on Star, the smallest pony of the three. Star was a pure white Welsh mare built like a miniature Arabian horse. And on Megan's other side was Ruth-Ann, riding the tallest pony, Zipper. Zipper was a small sorrel and white Paint—so he was actually a small horse, not a pony.

Star and Kendra were both puffing slightly. Kendra's brown hair had slipped out from under her riding helmet and lay tangled down her neck; Star's normally snow-white sides were wet underneath her cinch. Only Zipper looked cool and refreshed, but Ruth-Ann looked as limp and tired as a worn-out beach towel.

"I'd be awfully surprised if Zipper passed out," Ruth-Ann said, patting her horse's neck. "I'm the one doing all the work!" She wiped a bead of perspiration from her forehead dramatically.

Megan knew how quiet and lazy Zipper could be, and she was thankful for once that Blondie wasn't quite that quiet. Sometimes Megan was a bit jealous of Ruth-Ann. Zipper never seemed to be frightened of anything, and there definitely were things that frightened Blondie. Things such as barking dogs— even little ones like Megan's neighbor's tiny Yorkshire terrier—and flags blowing in the wind and cows and water sprinklers and plastic garbage bags and . . .

But on days like today, when Zipper was hot and sweaty, he could be very, very lazy.

Only a dumb horse would work hard on a day like today, Zipper seemed to be thinking. And Zipper definitely was not a dumb horse! He knew how to open gates and untie ropes and pick up things with his teeth.

"I think we should start our lessons earlier next week," Kendra said.

"It's just too hot at this time of the day," Megan agreed.

"My dad says this is the hottest July he's ever seen," Kendra continued. "And he says that he's over a hundred years old, so he's seen a lot of Julys."

"Your dad isn't a hundred years old," Ruth-Ann exclaimed.

"I know," Kendra said. "But he says that some days he feels that old, raising a horse-crazy daughter!"

"Could we ride at nine o'clock next week?" Megan asked, turning to Trish. "It should still be fairly cool at that time of the day."

"Nine is too early!" Ruth-Ann complained.

"It isn't that early," Megan said. "And you live only a couple of miles away."

"You'd think it was early if you had a little brother like Mikey," Ruth-Ann replied. "He's awake every night fussing. Mom says he has a heat rash. I'm grumpy in this heat too, but I don't keep him awake!"

"When would you like to do our lessons?" Megan asked, looking at their instructor.

Trish sighed and pushed a lock of long hair out of her face. "Girls," she said. "I don't think we'll be having a lesson next week."

"No lesson? We don't have to ride at nine o'clock," Megan said quickly. "We can ride any time you want."

"I need to have a serious talk with all of you," Trish said. "But let's finish today's lesson before we get into that. OK?"

The Ready to Ride girls looked at each other and then nodded.

"I want to teach you how to sidepass," Trish said. "When you and your ponies learn how to sidepass, you'll be able to control where they put each of their feet. You will turn more smoothly and be able to move your horse's head one direction while their feet go in another."

"Why would I want my horse's head moving a different direction than her feet?" Megan asked with a grin. She pictured falling into thin air while Blondie's front half trotted to the right and her back half trotted to the left!

"Sidepassing is a very useful tool," Trish said. "Show jumpers need to sidepass so they're in line for the jumps. Western riders need to sidepass for flying lead changes. Even trail riders use sidepassing to go around obstacles or over narrow bridges. So pay attention for another few minutes, OK? We're just about finished for the day."

Trish showed the girls how to pull back and apply pressure to the reins to stop their ponies from walking forward, while at the same time lifting one leg to create an "open door" and using their opposite leg to press on the pony's ribcage.

Within a few minutes, Kendra had Star sidepassing smoothly along the arena fence. "I suspect your sister trained Star to sidepass before you owned her," Trish said. "So that makes your job a lot easier."

But neither Blondie nor Zipper understood what they were being asked to do, as they tried to move ahead to relieve the pressure and yet were held back by the reins.

At first Zipper was confused, then he became frustrated. Soon he decided that he wasn't going to move at all. He stood firmly planted in the arena, ignoring Ruth-Ann's bumping heels as she tried to get him to step to the right.

Blondie was confused and frustrated too. But she didn't stand still like Zipper. Instead she began to bob her head up and down crossly, making her long blond mane snap back and forth. And when Megan continued to follow Trish's instructions to apply firmer pressure with her right leg, Blondie began to fidget. She pranced forward a step and then backwards. She threw her head into the air and jerked on the reins, trying to pull them out of Megan's hands. She even raised her foot in front of her and pawed crossly, snorting impatiently once or twice.

Megan was just about to quit pushing with

her leg and to tell Trish that she really didn't want to learn to sidepass after all, when Blondie did it! She took one smooth step sideways.

"Perfect!" Trish exclaimed. "Let loose with the reins and stop pushing with your leg."

Megan relaxed the reins, and Blondie sighed and lowered her head.

"Remember, girls," Trish said. "It isn't the cue that trains your horse; it's the relief of the cue. The quicker you reward your animal for doing the correct thing by taking away the pressure, the quicker she will understand what you're asking."

"Can I try again?" Megan asked.

Trish nodded. "Go the same direction," she said. "You need to teach your horse to move one direction well before you train her to go the other way." Megan pushed her right leg firmly into Blondie's golden side again and raised her left leg, so Blondie was free to move that direction. This time she had to push only a few times before Blondie took another hesitant step to the side.

"Excellent," Trish said. "And Megan, can you see why it was important that you didn't quit when Blondie was throwing her head and acting grumpy? If you quit when she behaves badly, it's almost as though you're rewarding her bad behavior."

The woman turned and began to help Ruth-Ann with Zipper. She showed Ruth-Ann how to swing her leg with more strength when Zipper was ignoring her. "Sometimes you have to be quite forceful with really quiet horses," Trish said. "Just remember to reward Zipper's slightest response." Finally Zipper took a step to the side and then another.

When the girls were finished, they dismounted and led the ponies over to the nearby hitching rail. Trish followed them, helping each girl as they unsaddled their ponies and brushed their sweaty backs.

"So tell us about the riding lessons," Megan finally said.

"You said you had something serious to talk about," Kendra reminded her. "Aren't you going to teach lessons anymore?"

Trish sighed. "Girls," she said slowly, "I won't be able to teach anyone riding lessons for at least a month. Maybe even longer."

"No lessons for a whole month!" Ruth-Ann exclaimed. "But summer holidays are the best time to ride!"

"Is something wrong?" Megan asked.

"I have some bad news," Trish said. "Some very bad news. The doctors say I have cancer."

Something Is Wrong With Trish!

"You have cancer?" Megan wondered if she'd heard Trish correctly.

"How can you have cancer?" Kendra asked. "Only really old people get cancer."

Trish smiled faintly. "People of all ages can have cancer," she said, "even if they aren't really old."

"What kind of cancer do you have?"

"What can the doctors do?"

"How did you find out?"

"Are you going to have an operation?"

The questions tumbled out.

"Are you going to . . ." Ruth-Ann started to ask and then stopped.

Megan knew that the rest of the sentence—the unspoken part—had been, *Are you going to die?* Her stomach suddenly felt odd with a heavy, sick feeling, like the one she got when her parents' car swooped over a bump in the road. Trish was more than their riding instructor. She was their friend! She had taught them all how to ride better, and she had helped them solve a lot of pony problems. All three girls phoned her sometimes, just to talk, even if it wasn't about horses!

And Trish had taught them all about Jesus' love in a way that other people hadn't seemed to do. So how could God let someone like Trish have cancer?

"Sit down," Trish said, "and I'll tell you everything I know." The three girls sank down into the prickly summer grass, while Trish pulled up a lawn chair.

They were all silent for a moment. The only sound Megan could hear was the swish of Blondie's tail as she chased away a persistent horsefly.

"I have cancer in my left breast," Trish finally said. "I found a lump there a month ago and went to my doctor."

"You have cancer in your breast?" Megan asked.

"Don't say that word," Kendra said. "It isn't polite."

Trish smiled a bit wider this time. "Girls," she said, "there isn't anything wrong with the word *breast*. God made all the parts of our bodies, you know. A breast is just a part of us—like a knee or an elbow."

"I know," Kendra said, "but we don't talk about some parts."

"Well, maybe not in public," Trish agreed. "At least, not all the time. But when it comes to our health, we need to take care of all our parts, even the private ones."

"I have a dumb question," Megan said slowly. "How do you know the lump is cancer? Can't lumps be something else?"

"Yes, they can," Trish said. "Women are supposed to check their breasts every month for lumps or changes. Last month I found a little bump that never used to be there. My doctor could feel it too, so she sent me to the hospital for a special X-ray. It showed that there was something suspicious there. I've had some more tests, and the doctors have decided for sure that the lump is cancerous."

"You let your doctor see your breast?" Kendra screwed up her face. "That's awful."

"Kendra," Trish said, "it would be even more awful if I had a problem and didn't let my doctor help."

"Some people die of cancer," Ruth-Ann stated bluntly.

"Some types of cancer can be fixed," Megan said. "My Grandma Carter had skin cancer on her face last year, and she had to have a whole bunch of radiation on it. Now the cancer is totally gone."

"That's right," Trish said. "Next week I'll have an operation to remove the lump from my breast. I won't be able to ride or teach lessons for at least a month, maybe longer. Dr. Smythe will check the lump for bad cells, and then she will decide if I need radiation or medicine to make the cancer stay away."

Blondie picked that moment to let out a big horse sneeze. "Yuck!" Megan exclaimed, wiping little droplets of horse spit off her arm. "You are so gross, Blondie!"

"Blondie and Star are girl horses," Kendra said, looking at the two small mares. "Can horses get breast cancer, too?"

Trish laughed. "Trust a Ready to Ride girl to think of a question like that!" she chuckled. "Always thinking about their horses! Well, I've heard of girl dogs having breast cancer, so I suppose a girl horse could too."

"How can you laugh?" Megan burst out. "If I had cancer, I'd be scared to death!"

"I *am* scared, Megan," Trish said softly. "But I decided a long time ago that God is in charge of my life. Bad things could happen anytime! I could fall off a horse and be hurt, but I don't quit riding. Instead, I wear my helmet and try to take care of myself, and then I leave the rest up to God. I could have a car accident, but instead of not driving I wear my seat belt and drive carefully. And that's how I feel about my cancer. I'm going to a good doctor, and I'm going to follow her advice. I'll pray about it lots too. Then I'm going to try to leave the rest in God's hands."

"You're so brave," Megan said.

"Trusting God isn't being brave," Trish said. "It's being smart. He knows so much more than I do. So I'm going to trust Him even when things look awful around me."

"Why does God let good people get cancer?" Ruth-Ann wanted to know.

"Satan is at war with God," Trish said. "And sometimes good people get hurt. But don't forget, even if bad things do happen here, God is still going to win the war. I want to be on God's side, because He has so much planned for people who love Him."

Soon Trish excused herself. The three girls were quieter than usual as they put the ponies out into their paddock.

Megan watched as Blondie walked straight to the middle of her pen and pawed the dusty ground. Her legs buckled under her as she flopped onto her side and began to roll back and forth. Her little amber legs waved merrily in the air as the pony rolled from one side to the other, scratching each sweaty spot until she was satisfied.

Blondie was delighted to be finished with her work. She didn't have any worries; she would have the rest of the hot day off to munch delicious grass or just stand around and relax. Blondie's biggest worry would be horseflies!

But Megan had a really big worry now.

Maybe Trish didn't feel really scared about cancer. But Megan sure did.

She loved Trish. There had to be something she could do. But what? What could a ten-year-old girl do to help someone with a big—no, a gigantic—problem like cancer?

It seemed like a problem too big even for the Ready to Ride Club to solve.

The Ready to Ride Club Has an Idea

The R2R Club met early the next morning at the Lewises' farm. They had decided to take their ponies for a trail ride and discuss Trish's big problem. The girls had solved many different problems before by talking about things together. Perhaps today they could think of a way to help Trish.

"Mom sent some sunscreen," Megan said. She put a dab of lotion on her hand and rubbed it carefully onto her face.

Kendra and Ruth-Ann also applied lotion to their faces and arms. All three girls were wearing pants, even in the summer heat, since they knew their legs would rub on their saddles if they rode in shorts. "Can I put some sunscreen on Zipper's nose?" Ruth-Ann asked. "I won't use too much."

"Sunscreen on Zipper's nose?"

"Look," Ruth-Ann said, pointing at her pony. They all peered at Zipper's face. Zipper had a "bald" face, similar to many other Paint horses. (A horse with a lot of white hair on its face is said to have a "bald" or "bonnet" face; it isn't really bald!) The places on Zipper's face that were normally pale pink were now dark red and slightly cracked.

"People can get sunburns in this heat," Ruth-Ann said, "and so can horses."

"That looks sore," Kendra said. Then she turned and looked at Star. "Star has white hair on her whole head," she said thoughtfully, "but she doesn't burn. I wonder why."

"I know the answer," Ruth-Ann said. "Remember, Star wasn't born white, she was born dark. Her skin is dark under all her white hair, so it's tough and doesn't burn easily. But Zipper has some skin that's dark and some skin that's light pink. The pink skin is what gets sunburned."

"That makes sense," Megan agreed. She thought about Star's registered name—A Perfect Star. No one understood how a solid white pony without a visible star could have a name like that, but Megan had seen photos of Kendra's older sister on Star years ago. At that time, the pony was dark gray with four white stockings and a perfect white star.

Zipper wasn't enthusiastic about the sunscreen and lifted his head, so Ruth-Ann had to stand on tiptoe to reach his muzzle. The expression on Zipper's face said *Yuck!* and *Gross!* and *You people are so dumb, but I still love you*, while he raised his head and moved his nose from side to side, trying to avoid the lotion. Finally Ruth-Ann was able to coat the worst of the red places with the sunscreen, and she passed the tube back to Megan with thanks.

"Look what my mom bought me at the tack store yesterday," Kendra said. "She told me I'd need it if we keep riding in this awful heat!"

Kendra held up a plastic container with a flowery purple cloth cover and loop.

"What is it?" Ruth-Ann asked. "Fancy suntan lotion?"

"It's a water bottle," Megan said, wishing she had thought to bring one herself. With this heat, she'd probably be thirsty before they even started their ride.

"It isn't a water bottle," Kendra said. "It's a canteen. Mom says cowboys used canteens years ago, especially when they went on long cattle drives. See, this part fastens around the horn, and then there are strings to tie it to the front of the saddle so it doesn't bounce when we trot or lope."

"Oh, sure," Megan said. "I'll bet a lot of cowboys carried pretty purple canteens."

"With flowers," Ruth-Ann agreed.

"And they probably curled their hair before they put on their cowboy hats," Megan continued.

"I wonder if they used fancy perfume to cover the smell of stinky cows," Ruth-Ann said thoughtfully.

Kendra laughed. "That's right," she said, hanging the canteen by its loop from her saddle horn. "We'll see who makes fun of my canteen when we're all dying for a drink of nice, cool water!"

"I wasn't making fun of your water bottle," Megan said quickly. "I was admiring it."

"Yeah," Ruth-Ann said, "me, too. And I think the purple is lovely. Any cowboy would want a canteen just like it!"

Before long, the girls were riding down an old, deserted dirt road at a steady trot. Tall trees towered on both sides of the road and threw a comfortable shade across their paths.

"Whew!" Megan sighed when they finally pulled their ponies down to a walk. "It's hard to believe it could be this hot at ten-thirty."

"It will be worse once we get off this road and in the open," Kendra said.

"But then we'll get back to the shade before long," Ruth-Ann said. "So we'll be OK."

They continued at a steady pace, trotting the horses for a while and then bringing them back to a walk to catch their breath, before trotting some more.

"Blondie loves trail riding," Megan said. She guided the little mare to the right, avoiding a big rock that lay directly in their path. It was true. Blondie was always a willing horse in the riding ring, but she really seemed the happiest when they were riding in the open. She always kept her neck nicely arched as a proper Morgan would, and her little fox ears pricked back and forth cheerfully as she watched everything around her. Blondie's ground-covering trot could travel miles effortlessly.

Just then, there was a flutter of wings as a pair of prairie chickens flew up from the long grass at the edge of the road. Zipper was the pony nearest the birds, but he didn't break stride except to bob his head quickly at the strange sound before continuing on.

Blondie and Star were both startled by the loud noise of the prairie chickens' wings. Star jumped one step sideways and then settled down. But Blondie moved much quicker and farther. She bounded three or four steps across the road, moving so fast that Megan had to grab a handful of long mane to keep from falling off. But before Megan could pull on the reins, Blondie seemed to realize what the noise was. *Whoops!* her ears seemed to say. *Not a monster, just a noisy bird. My mistake.* In a moment, they were all back to a relaxed trot.

Before long, they moved out of the cool trees and into the horrible summer heat. Megan couldn't help glancing at Kendra and her new water bottle.

Ruth-Ann seemed to be thinking the same thing, because in a moment she said, "That sure is a lovely, lovely cowboy canteen you have there, Kendra. Very authentic looking."

"I wish I had one just like it," Megan agreed.

"That purple looks perfect on Star," Ruth-Ann continued.

Kendra reached over and lifted the canteen from the saddle horn. She drooped the reins around Star's neck, and while they continued to walk, she carefully unscrewed the lid from her canteen. "I sure hope the water is still nice and cold," she said with a small sigh. She lifted the container to her mouth and then paused before drinking. "Actually, I'm not that thirsty," she said. She poured a little water onto her hand and patted it on her forehead. "But that certainly is refreshing." Kendra started to screw the lid back onto the canteen.

"Oh, dear R2R friend," Ruth-Ann begged, "I'm really thirsty. Do you think I could have a little drink?"

"A drink?" Kendra asked. "Out of this canteen? I thought you didn't like it."

"Just a tiny little swallow?" Ruth-Ann begged. "So small you won't even miss it?"

"Me, too, please," Megan said. "I feel like a baked potato sizzling in the oven!"

"Of course you can have a drink," Kendra said. She passed the canteen to Ruth-Ann with a grin. "I'm just teasing you!"

Ruth-Ann pulled Zipper to a halt and unscrewed the lid from the canteen again. Then with an eager look, she tipped the water bottle back and took a big swallow. Ruth-Ann swallowed once and then a strange expression crossed her face before she swallowed again. "Yu-uu-ckkk!" she exclaimed. She wrinkled up her face and passed the bottle to Megan.

Megan looked at Kendra, wondering if she was playing a trick on them, but the expression on Kendra's face was one of confusion and surprise. Megan took a small sip of water. It tasted horrible! The liquid was warm as bath water and had a strong plastic taste. "Did you wash the canteen before you used it?" Megan asked.

Kendra shook her head and took the canteen back from Megan. She took a small sip and then spit the water over Star's shoulder. "That's awful," she agreed.

"No wonder cowboys always looked so rough and shabby!" Ruth-Ann laughed. "Their water was too awful to drink."

"When you get home, you should wash your canteen with lots of soapy water," Megan advised. "That should make it better."

When they were off the narrow path and back into the shade of the pasture, the girls began to talk. "What can the Ready to Ride Club do to help Trish?" Ruth-Ann wondered out loud.

"I thought about that all night long," Kendra said. "But since we aren't doctors or nurses, I don't think there's anything we can do."

"We can pray," Megan said.

"Of course," Kendra said. "I'm praying already. But there must be something more!"

"We can ask our church to pray for her," Ruth-Ann suggested.

"My mom said the ladies of the church have already started a prayer chain for Trish," Kendra said.

"But what can *we* do?" Megan asked. "I want to do something special to help."

"We could buy her some flowers when she's in the hospital," Ruth-Ann suggested.

"Flowers are OK," Megan said, "but they won't help Trish get better."

"The ponies could send her a bouquet of carrots," Ruth-Ann said. "That would be cute."

"Cute," Megan agreed, "but still not very helpful."

"What helps people get better when they have cancer?" Kendra asked.

"Nothing," Ruth-Ann replied.

"That isn't true," Megan said. "Radiation helped my grandma."

"I don't even know what radiation is," Ruth-Ann said.

"It's like X-rays, I think," Megan said. "They use the X-rays to kill the bad cancer cells. But first, they have to decide whether or not that type of cancer can be hurt by radiation. And then they have to decide where to put the radiation and for how long."

"Doctors must spend a lot of time learning about cancer," Kendra said.

"My mom says that years ago almost everyone who had cancer died," Megan replied. "Now many people get better because scientists have found new ways to treat cancer."

"My parents always give money to the Cancer Society," Ruth-Ann said. "Their research helps the doctors know what to do."

"We could give some money to the Cancer

Society," Ruth-Ann said. "That would be a way to help people like Trish."

"But we're just kids," Kendra said. "We don't have very much money."

Megan didn't say anything. Instead she swatted a mosquito that lingered around her leg, and thought for a moment. She had seen a notice in the local paper last week, but it hadn't seemed very important at the time. Suddenly she knew it was important. It was something that could help people with cancer, like Trish. And it was something the Ready to Ride Club could do.

There was going to be a Cancer Trail Ride at Hardisty next week. The girls could get pledges and earn money for cancer research. And they could do it while riding their ponies!

Earning Money for the Big Trail Ride

"Of course I'll help you," Megan's mother said. She phoned the newspaper office that very afternoon and asked for information about the trail ride. The newspaper office soon faxed back a pledge form and a fact sheet. "And I will be your very first donor," Mrs. Lewis said. She wrote her name and address on the top line of the form, and beside it she wrote in big numbers —$40.

"That's a lot of money!" Megan said.

"Yes, it is," Mrs. Lewis agreed. "But I want to help in the fight against cancer. I've always felt that way, but since Grandma Carter had cancer I'm even more interested in the disease."

It seemed to Megan that earning money for the Cancer Trail Ride wasn't going to be very difficult if people were all as generous as her mom!

"I do have one concern though," Mrs. Lewis said thoughtfully.

"What?"

"I don't think you should take Blondie on the Cancer Trail Ride," Mrs. Lewis said. "She is a lively pony and might get very excited and difficult to handle. I wouldn't want you to have problems."

"Blondie's a wonderful trail horse!" Megan protested. "And I ride with Kendra and Ruth-Ann all the time. Blondie's always good."

"Yes," Mrs. Lewis said. "But riding with two horses in familiar places isn't the same as a busy cancer ride. The newspaper man told me there were a hundred horses and riders last year."

"We'll keep out of their way," Megan said. "I won't let anything hurt Blondie."

"I'd like you to ride Seeker," Mrs. Lewis replied, referring to Blondie's mother. "Seeker's been on big trail rides before, and she'll stay relaxed."

"Mom!" Megan said. "I won't have any problems. I'll have Ruth-Ann and Kendra to keep me company, and we're all good riders. You said so yourself."

"You are excellent riders," Mrs. Lewis agreed. "And I'm very proud of the three of you. But you're only ten years old. You could have all sorts of trouble, and who would help you? Please think seriously about taking Seeker instead of Blondie."

Megan did not want to take Seeker. Seeker was a lovely Palomino Morgan mare, but she was about twenty-eight years old now and had mild arthritis. Sometimes her legs bothered her, and she would limp if she trotted or cantered very far. How could Megan ride the long trail on a lame horse?

Besides, Megan didn't love Seeker. She loved Blondie. She wanted to ride her own horse. But first, she needed to get more people to sign her donor form.

By evening Megan had fourteen different

pledges on her form. Some people had donated only two or three dollars, but most had donated quite a bit more. Megan used her dad's calculator and found that she already had $234!

And I still have a lot more people to ask, Megan thought to herself. There was Mrs. Boris, their nearest neighbor, and her uncle Sam and her school bus driver, Mr. Foxworthy. And she could ask Pastor Bob and maybe Mrs. Rowdosky, her Sabbath School teacher. Why, she could earn hundreds of dollars for cancer research! And then there would be all the money that Ruth-Ann and Kendra would earn too.

The girls talked about nothing but the cancer ride when they worked their ponies the next morning. "I'm going to take my canteen," Kendra said, "because it's sure to be really warm on the long trail ride."

"You're going to drink that awful water?" Ruth-Ann asked, wrinkling up her nose.

"It's much better now," Kendra reassured them. "Mom and I washed the canteen really well with soapy water, and we even put some lemon juice in it for a while."

"Lemon juice?" Ruth-Ann asked.

"To take out that nasty plastic taste," Kendra said. "It really helped."

"We'll need to take a few other things with us," Megan said. "The newspaper man said that a barbecue supper would be provided for all the riders, but we're supposed to pack our own sack lunch."

"Guess what?" Ruth-Ann said. "They're going to award prizes to some of the riders at the supper."

"Prizes for what?" Megan asked.

"One for the oldest rider and one for the youngest," Ruth-Ann said. "And there are prizes for the riders who earn the most money too."

Megan thought about the money she had already earned and how many more people she wanted to ask. Maybe she could earn a prize on the Cancer Trail Ride!

"I'm going to take cheese buns for lunch," Kendra said. "And a juice box."

"And I want to take some bug spray," Ruth-Ann said.

"And my sunscreen," Megan said.

"And a hoof pick," Kendra added. "In case, one of the ponies gets a rock stuck in his feet."

"I want a water bottle of my own," Megan said. She wondered how she would carry all those supplies with her: a lunch and water bottle and sunscreen and bug spray. That would take a backpack to carry, but she didn't know how easy it would be to ride with a backpack on her back.

Megan's grandmother solved her problem the very next day, by appearing at the door carrying a surprise. "I wanted to do something for my girl who's going on the cancer ride," she said. "Your mom thought this would be useful."

Megan unwrapped a long, slim nylon bag. The bag had a zipper down its entire length and two metal D rings on one side. Megan looked at the bag. She unzipped the zipper and looked inside. She tried to imagine what the bag was for.

Suddenly Megan knew. It was a modern type of saddlebag. It was made to go behind a

Western saddle. The long leather strings on her saddle would tie onto the bag's metal D rings. The bag wasn't big, but it was large enough to easily carry a lunch and water bottle and a hoof pick.

"And put Grandpa and me down for a hundred dollars," Grandma Carter said.

"One hundred dollars!" Megan exclaimed.

"I always donate to the Cancer Society," Grandma said. "This year I'll give a bit extra. I'm proud of all the hard work you girls are doing to help Trish and me and other people with cancer."

Megan hugged her grandmother and then hurried off to figure out the latest total for her donations. Thanks to Grandma's money and another generous pledge from a nurse who worked with her mother, Megan had already earned over $350!

I'll bet I've already earned more money than most people, Megan thought with a smile. *This is perfect. I'm earning money for doing something I love, and I might even win a prize at the same time! And we're doing this for Trish.*

Final Preparations

Trish had her surgery on Tuesday. Later that evening Megan begged to be taken to the hospital to visit her friend.

"No," Mrs. Lewis said firmly. "You need to give Trish a few days to recover."

"But the trail ride is in two days!" Megan moaned. "And I need to see her before then."

"Why don't you phone the hospital and ask how she's doing?" Megan's father suggested.

Mrs. Lewis shook her head. "The nurses won't tell you anything," she said, "because of confidentiality."

"What!"

"Don't be upset," Mrs. Lewis said. "Nurses aren't allowed to say anything about their patients."

"But I'm worried," Megan said.

"Why don't you phone and ask Pastor Bob?" Mr. Lewis said. "He was going to stop by the hospital today."

"That's a good idea," Mrs. Lewis said. "Pastor Bob is such a nice man." Megan's parents did not attend church very often, but they always enjoyed talking with the pastor, and he seemed to enjoy talking to them.

Megan bounded over to the phone and dialed the pastor's number. She was smiling when she got off the phone a few minutes later.

"Good news?" Mrs. Lewis asked.

"Pastor Bob said Trish was sitting in bed, eating a muffin, when he stopped to visit," Megan said. "Her sister from New Mexico was there, and they were both very cheerful."

"That's good." Mrs. Lewis said.

"And guess what Trish did in the hospital today!"

"Had surgery?"

"Mom!" Megan said. "I know she had surgery. But what else do you think she did?"

"I don't know," Mrs. Lewis said. "I don't suppose she rode a horse?"

"Almost!" Megan exclaimed. "She told all the nurses and doctors about the Ready to Ride Club and how we're taking our ponies to the Hardisty Cancer Trail Ride. Pastor Bob said she earned another hundred dollars in pledges for me!"

"That much money?"

Megan giggled. "The doctor told Pastor Bob that Trish was telling everyone about the ride even when she was lying on the operating table. He thinks they agreed to pay her just so she'd be quiet, and they could put her to sleep and get on with the operation!"

"That's amazing," Mrs. Lewis said. "I think I would have been too scared to think about anything except my surgery."

"And Pastor Bob said she really doesn't want people buying flowers for her," Megan continued. "She said she'd rather the money that would be spent on flowers go to the trail ride instead."

"Really?"

"She told Pastor Bob that flowers aren't important to her," Megan said. "She said that people were much more important. She's met some other ladies in the hospital who have cancer, and she wants to help them and everyone else who has cancer."

"Well," Mr. Lewis said, "are you ready for the Cancer Trail Ride?"

"Almost," Megan said. "I have my saddlebag packed, and I have my pledge form and permission sheet filled out. I even washed my saddle pad, so it'll be comfortable for Blondie."

"I was hoping you'd ride Seeker," Mrs. Lewis said slowly.

"Mom, Blondie will be fine," Megan assured her.

"I can't get the day off from work to ride with you," Mrs. Lewis said. "So I'm going to ask Mandy if she'll go with you girls."

"Mandy shouldn't miss work," Megan said. "She's saving money for college."

"I read the rules carefully last night," Mrs. Lewis explained, "and it says that all riders under the age of sixteen must be accompanied by an adult."

"Mandy isn't an adult," Megan said. "She's a big sister."

"She's a big sister who just turned eighteen," Mrs. Lewis said. "So she's officially an adult. And Mandy can earn some extra money for the Cancer Society, so that will be a good thing."

Early Wednesday morning, the three girls hurried out to the farm to exercise their ponies. But first they decided to clean the ponies thoroughly so they'd be beautiful for their big day tomorrow.

"Look how filthy Zipper is!" Ruth-Ann moaned as she tied the little Paint to the sturdy hitching post. She grabbed a soft body brush and began flicking muck and dirt off Zipper's back. Puffs of dust rose off Zipper's rump with every swipe of the brush.

"He's a real pig," Megan agreed, tying Blondie nearby.

"It's horrible!" Ruth-Ann said. She brushed harder. Zipper sighed and closed his eyes as though enjoying the nice massage. "How could he get this dirty?"

"The same way Star did," Kendra said, leading Star up behind them. She snapped the mare's lead rope into place and sighed. "And Star's white, so every dirty spot is obvious!" The small Welsh mare was covered with grime and an enormous green stain crossed her right hip—even her flowing mane and tail were littered with small twigs and branches.

"It looks like they rolled in a garbage pile," Ruth-Ann said.

"Or worse," Kendra added.

"You're lucky," Ruth-Ann said, turning to Megan. "Blondie is such a tidy horse."

Megan nodded. Blondie did keep herself clean most of the time. Even now there were only faint traces of dust on Blondie's back. Megan quickly brushed Blondie's coat and then picked up a currycomb. She carefully went through Blondie's long mane and tail, removing any bits of grass or straw, and combing out each knot. Blondie stood patiently while the girl combed and curried and even trimmed the long hairs under her chin.

"There," Megan said, finally standing back to admire her work. "She looks nice enough to go to a horse show tomorrow instead of just a trail ride."

Megan had always loved Palomino colored horses. And Blondie was a perfect example of a Palomino. Her coat was a rich golden color, and her mane and tail were a thick, creamy accent. The little mare had four white socks, and even her eyelashes were a lovely golden tone.

Ruth-Ann and Kendra were still working energetically on their ponies. Megan kissed the tip of Blondie's velvety nose and then picked up a currycomb to help her friends.

Finally all three ponies were clean enough to satisfy the group.

The girls saddled up and headed into the nearby arena for a short ride. It was terribly hot by then, so they didn't ride for too long. "Just long enough to get the kinks out of the ponies' legs," Megan announced.

"I'm going to pray that it isn't this hot tomorrow," Ruth-Ann decided.

"Do you think it's OK to pray for things like that?" Megan asked.

"Of course," Ruth-Ann said. "The Bible tells us to pray for all things."

"I guess you're right," Megan said. "But a hot day doesn't seem that important."

"You say that only because you've never dropped over unconscious with heat exhaustion!" Kendra laughed.

"Have you?"

"Of course not," Kendra said. "But it doesn't sound like fun."

"My mom told me it's not supposed to be this hot tomorrow," Ruth-Ann said.

"Let's hope not," Megan replied. "In fact, a breeze would be nice too. It would cool us down, and it would keep the horseflies away."

"Then I'll pray for that too," Ruth-Ann said confidently.

The girls had just finished putting the ponies back into the pasture when a small car whirled down the driveway and pulled up nearby. It was Megan's sister, Mandy.

"Hi girls!" Mandy called. "Are your ponies ready for tomorrow?"

"We're all set," Ruth-Ann said. "Are you coming with us?"

Mandy nodded her head. "I just want to make sure that Seeker's ready for the long ride," she said. "And I need to clean my tack too." With a quick wave, the older girl grabbed a halter and headed across the paddock for the Morgan mare.

"Why is Mandy riding Seeker tomorrow?" Kendra asked. "Doesn't she have her own horse?"

"Her show horse, Luna, isn't used to trail rides," Megan said.

"But Seeker's getting old," Ruth-Ann said. "I hope the ride doesn't hurt her."

"My mom says Mandy will be walking Seeker all the way," Megan reassured her friends. "So it shouldn't hurt her."

"I'm glad Mandy's coming with us," Kendra said. "And my dad's glad too, since he can't ride."

"It would be fun if your dad came with us," Megan said with a grin. Mr. Rawling was famous for his constant jokes, and the girls all enjoyed being around him.

"Don't worry," Kendra said. "He agreed to drive us there tomorrow. That should be enough."

The girls stacked their saddles, blankets, and bridles into the horse trailer, while Mandy brushed Seeker. They had finished packing as Mandy began to lead the big horse in a slow circle around her.

Megan watched her sister for a moment. She didn't mind if Mandy came on the trail ride. Mandy was a super big sister, and Seeker was always a well-behaved horse.

Megan was certain she wouldn't need her sister's help tomorrow. Blondie was going to be good, as always. That was her name after all—Good as Gold Blondie! But Mandy had managed to fill most of her donation form with pledges, and that was great. The more money they earned, the better it would be for the researchers who were studying cancer.

And the better that would be for Trish!

And best of all, Megan's own pledge form was full; she had even needed to start a second one. She had over $560 in donations!

Megan wondered how many riders had earned that much money. She was quite pleased with herself. Fund-raising was fun. Tomorrow was going to be wonderful. What could be better than a trail ride on Blondie with her R2R friends? And she stood a very good chance of winning a prize for all her pledges!

Megan could hardly wait.

A Stormy Thursday Morning

"Heigh-ho! Heigh-ho! It's off to ride we go!" The three girls sang loudly in the backseat of the crowded one-ton diesel truck.

Mr. Rawling and Mandy rolled their eyes at each other, and then Mr. Rawling broke into a song of his own. "I owe! I owe!" he sang off-key, "So it's off to work I go!"

The girls grinned at each other and peered out the foggy truck windows. The weather this morning was very different than it had been for the last few weeks. For one thing, the sun, which normally shone brilliantly, was now draped in clouds. A gusty wind blew dust across the road, making the early morning seem even darker.

"We might even get some rain out of this," Mr. Rawling said. "Won't that be terrific?"

"Terrific," Kendra said, "except not today."

"This bad weather is all your fault," Megan said, turning to look at Ruth-Ann.

"This is Ruth-Ann's fault?" Mr. Rawling asked, glancing at the backseat. "I should have known."

"Daddy!" Kendra exclaimed.

"Did you do a rain dance?" Mr. Rawling asked. "That's supposed to work."

"I don't know any rain dances, Mr. Rawling," Ruth-Ann giggled.

"Well, then how did a young lady such as yourself cause such horrible weather?" he asked.

"She prayed," Megan said.

"You prayed for a storm?" Mr. Rawling asked. "That's what I like to see—a girl that isn't scared of bad weather!"

Ruth-Ann frowned. "I didn't exactly pray for a storm," she said.

"Well, what did you pray for then?"

"I prayed that it wouldn't be so hot today," Ruth-Ann admitted.

"Aha!"

"And she prayed for a breeze," Kendra said.

A plastic bag suddenly blew out of the nearby ditch and tumbled across the road directly in front of the truck and horse trailer. "Wow," Mandy said. "And my friends think that prayer doesn't work!"

"Is it too late to pray for something new?" Ruth-Ann asked meekly from her seat.

"Pray that I become a half-a-millionaire," Mr. Rawling suggested.

"A half-a-millionaire?" Megan asked. "What's that?"

"Well," Mr. Rawling said. "I figure that when Ruth-Ann prays for something she gets twice as much as she asks for. So I need her to pray for only half a million, and I'll become a millionaire!"

"Daddy, you know God doesn't answer prayers that way," Kendra said.

"I know," Mr. Rawling admitted. "Sometimes God answers prayers 'Yes.' Sometimes He answers them 'No,' and sometimes He says 'Wait.' By the end of today we'll know how

He answered Ruth-Ann's prayer about weather, I guess."

Soon they arrived at the Hardisty Fair Grounds. Dozens of stock trailers were already parked on the thick grass. Horses were everywhere—some tied to trailers, others being led or ridden around the area by their owners.

Megan saw horses of every color and size. Several small children, barely more than toddlers, were on tiny ponies being led by parents. A couple, who looked old enough to be Megan's grandparents, was riding at a relaxed walk together. There were black horses, sorrel horses, bay horses, gray horses, spotted horses. Everywhere she looked there were more and more and more horses!

"Wow! It's crowded already," Megan said. She felt a sudden shiver of nervousness cross her spine, and she took a deep breath to calm herself.

Megan knew that most horses don't like stormy weather. Windy days can make the calmest horse become jumpy and nervous. Normally, Blondie behaved fine at home, even on a stormy day. But here, in the crowd of unfamiliar horses, things might suddenly be very different.

"I didn't expect so many people," Mr. Rawling said, stopping the truck. "I thought the bad weather would keep some people at home."

"We couldn't stay home," Ruth-Ann said. "Otherwise we wouldn't earn all the money that people have pledged to us."

"We want to do this for Trish," Megan said. "It's important."

Mr. Rawling looked serious for once as he undid his seat belt. "It's important that you girls keep safe today too," he said. "We don't need another person lying in a hospital bed beside Trish."

"I'll take care of them, Mr. Rawling," Mandy said.

"I'm sure you'll be a big help," Mr. Rawling said. "But I know Someone who's an even better help. And that's God. I think we should pray for His protection today."

No one complained as Mr. Rawling bowed his head and prayed for the safety of everyone involved in the Cancer Trail Ride. He said all four girls' names out loud—Mandy and Megan and Ruth-Ann and Kendra—and he even prayed for the four horses: Seeker, Blondie, Zipper, and Star.

Megan felt a bit better.

"And put on your riding helmets," Mr. Rawling said. "You want to protect your brains."

"I thought you said girls didn't have brains, Daddy," Kendra teased, picking up her hot pink helmet.

"You must have me mistaken with another mean father," Mr. Rawling said. "I always knew you girls had brains. I just didn't know if you used them as much as you should!"

"We always wear our helmets, Mr. Rawling," Megan said.

"Then I guess you are using your brain after all," Mr. Rawling replied.

Megan slid on her helmet and zipped her jacket to the top. She stepped outside. The nervousness reappeared as soon as she felt the sharp breeze against her face.

Mr. Rawling held the trailer door open while the girls unloaded the horses. Blondie didn't seem spooked, but she was a bit restless, and Megan was glad to tie her near Seeker, who stood quietly with a *been there, done that* attitude. Mr. Rawling took the four girls' pledge forms to the office while the Ready to Ride Club rushed around, trying to saddle and blanket their ponies.

"Help!" Ruth-Ann called from the other side of the truck.

"Is Zipper being a brat?" Megan asked. She could hardly imagine the normally calm young horse acting up, but in this wind anything seemed possible. She hurried behind the trailer.

Ruth-Ann was struggling to saddle Zipper. She had her new red saddle blanket neatly centered on his back, but every time she let go of the blanket and reached for her saddle, the wind blew the blanket right off the little Paint's back. Zipper didn't seem too startled by the flapping blanket, but Star, standing nearby, was gawking at the activity with wide eyes.

Megan held Zipper's blanket on his back as Ruth-Ann slipped the saddle into position. "Thanks," Ruth-Ann said. "I should be OK now."

Mandy helped Megan by holding Blondie's saddle pad in place and then quickly saddled Seeker while Megan pulled her saddle bag out of the back of the truck. "I get the impression that I won't need the sunscreen lotion today," Megan said. She dug in the bag and removed the container of lotion. The bag was lighter now, but still fairly bulky with Megan's bag lunch, a small water bottle, a hoof pick, and a container of horse treats.

She positioned the bag at the back of her Western saddle and carefully tied it into place with the saddle's long leather laces. Then Megan walked back to the truck and pulled out a pair of leather gloves and a head warmer that her mother had set aside earlier that day. "Mom thinks of everything," Megan said. She unbuckled her helmet, slipped the head warmer into place, and then pulled the helmet over it. It was a bit snug, but it would do. For once, Megan was glad her mother was such a worry-wart. The gloves and head warmer would make a big difference on today's windy ride.

Blondie Begins
the Ride

The trail ride was scheduled to begin at ten o'clock. Five minutes before ten, a man with a bullhorn walked to the center of the grassy lawn and began to make announcements at the top of his lungs. The wind seemed to blow some of the man's words away, but Megan was able to catch most of the instructions.

". . . You must not pass the trail boss, who is Mr. Erickson. He is riding a tall brown horse and wearing a bright orange fluorescent jacket . . ." The announcer pointed to a man on horseback at the edge of the crowd.

Blondie pawed the grass impatiently. She didn't seem to like still being tied to the stock trailer while many of the other horses were being ridden around the area.

". . . Will stop at approximately eleven-thirty for lunch. Make sure you bring your bag lunches as there will be no food or beverages supplied. There will be a corral where we stop to eat, so the horses can be tied to the wooden fencing. Make sure you bring a sturdy halter and rope with you if you want to tie your . . ."

Megan hadn't thought about bringing her halter and rope. Now she wondered whether it would be better to carry the halter or to tie it to her saddle. Perhaps she should just leave it on underneath Blondie's bridle.

"Supper will be back here at the Hardisty Hall," the announcer continued. Megan could hear better now. "We will eat at four o'clock. The barbecue is free for all riders who have earned at least fifty dollars on their pledge forms. Any family members who want to eat with us will be charged ten dollars for the food and drinks. Prizes will be awarded to riders after the barbecue."

Prizes! For a moment Megan had almost forgotten about the prizes. It seemed the goal was at least fifty dollars for each rider. Why, she had just over six hundred dollars now! That was more than ten times better!

A horse neighed loudly, and another horse whinnied back to it. Then the announcer finished his talk. "There are over a hundred and twenty horses here today. So remember to space yourselves out properly, so no one gets kicked. No dogs are allowed on the trail ride, so if you brought a dog, you must leave it tied to the trailer. If you must pass another horse, keep to a walk. Do not trot or canter past another horse. And really watch out for our young riders. Do what you can to keep everyone safe and happy. Good luck and be careful."

The man waved his arms, and a surge of riders started forward. The trail boss took the lead in his bright orange jacket. The Ready to Ride girls rushed back to the stock trailer and fumbled with their lead ropes, quickly trying to bridle their ponies.

Megan decided to leave Blondie's halter in place and just slide the bridle on top of everything. Blondie was normally easy to bridle, but today she was excited and distracted by the milling crowd of horses, and she flung her head into the air. Megan had to stand on tiptoe, but she was able to slip the bit into Blondie's mouth without any help. Then she double-checked that her cinch was tight and prepared to mount.

Blondie was worried that she was going to be left behind. She bobbed her head and circled Megan as the girl poked her toe into the stirrup, trying to mount. "Don't be such a silly goose," Megan muttered, pulling on the reins. "Star and Zipper and Seeker are here, waiting for you." But Blondie seemed more interested in all the strange horses that were streaming past her.

Finally Megan was able to get into the saddle. She felt a bit better when she saw that even the normally bombproof Zipper was wide-eyed and excited.

"Is everyone ready?" Mandy called.

Blondie tossed her head again and took a step forward, then a step backwards. Megan tightened the reins and nodded.

"Make sure we stay together," Mandy said. She squeezed Seeker into a walk, moving her slightly away from a group of horses right in front of her. "Once we're on the road the horses will calm down."

Mandy suggested that Blondie and Seeker walk side by side, with Zipper and Star following right behind them. "Horses feel comfortable being with their friends," Mandy said. "And let's make sure we keep a lot of space between us and the strange horses. This isn't a race."

Blondie didn't seem to know what to do. She walked beside Seeker for a while and then pranced sideways, watching a dark bay horse that was trying to pass on their left. Megan pulled on the reins to slow Blondie down and then moved her back beside Seeker. In a few minutes, they were on a well-mowed path, with a crowd of horse and riders both in front and behind them.

"How are you girls doing?" Mandy asked, twisting around in the saddle to look at Kendra and Ruth-Ann.

"Star's acting a bit silly," Kendra said.

"Zipper's OK," Ruth-Ann answered. "But he's walking a lot faster than normal."

"Most horses are a bit excited at the beginning of a crowded trail ride," Mandy said. "Just keep to a steady walk, and I expect they'll settle down soon."

Megan hoped so. But there was something about Blondie's attitude and the way she was moving that worried Megan. It almost felt as though she was riding a totally different horse. When she tried to turn Blondie the usual way, Blondie didn't respond. At first, she ignored the tug of the rein altogether, and then when she did turn, she did so in a jerky, darting motion. And instead of walking calmly, like normal, Blondie was jigging around in a funny little gait that was almost a walk and almost a trot.

Seeker appeared totally calm. Zipper, who normally walked so slowly that the group often had to stop and wait for him, was now walking so rapidly his nose was nearly on Seeker's tail. Even Star looked a bit worried. She snorted once or twice and swished her tail impatiently, but Kendra sat deeply in the saddle and appeared quite relaxed.

Within a few minutes, things began to change. Zipper took a deep breath and suddenly remembered that he really didn't like working too hard. His walk slowed down to his normal speed. Ruth-Ann's face became more relaxed, and she even began to smile.

Star was still walking fast, but she was no longer tossing her head. Kendra loosened her reins a bit more as the white mare began to unwind.

Seeker's golden ears flicked back and forth. She seemed to be trying to tell the ponies, *Don't worry, everything's OK. I've done this before, and you can too.*

Only Blondie was still acting silly. And instead of settling down, she was becoming more and more animated. The little jiggy trot was now becoming high and bouncy. When Megan pulled back on the reins, Blondie shook her head back and forth as though saying, *No, I won't obey.* And then she pranced even higher.

Megan's little saddlebag bounced up and down on Blondie's rump. It made more noise than Megan had expected; the water bottle and bug spray and lunch swished and rattled and thumped. Blondie didn't like the feeling, and she swished her tail and humped her back and complained about the sound for a moment.

Just then Star accidentally bumped into the back of Blondie, and the Palomino mare shot forward, almost unseating Megan. "Watch out!" Megan shouted at Kendra as she yanked on the reins.

"Sorry," Kendra called, but her voice was carried away by the wind as Blondie raced ahead. Megan turned Blondie in a circle and rode her back beside Seeker.

"Are you OK?" Mandy asked.

"I'm fine," Megan said through tight lips.

But she wasn't. Megan wasn't having any fun, and she was pretty sure that Blondie wasn't having any fun either. She had control of the little mare for the moment, but she didn't know how long it would last. And if Blondie acted any worse, Megan wouldn't be able to handle her.

Megan wondered if she should get off Blondie and lead her. But leading a prancing horse was difficult, and the path was crowded with dozens of other horses. If she were leading her, Megan worried that Blondie would step on her or knock her over in her excitement. No, leading didn't seem to be the answer.

The wind was horrible. It whipped down the narrow path and made Megan's eyes water. She wiped tears from her eyes with her sleeve and struggled to slow the mare down. At first she had just been afraid of Blondie. Now she was getting angry. Why was Blondie acting like this?

The next few minutes passed in a blur as Megan struggled to keep Blondie moving forward, and Blondie struggled to do everything else she could think of!

The scenery should have been beautiful. Instead Megan was only vaguely aware of trees and bushes rushing past her face.

"Would you like to ride Seeker?" Mandy finally asked. "We could trade horses."

"No!" Megan spat out. Blondie bounced in place, and the saddlebag rattled louder than ever. Megan could hear Ruth-Ann and Kendra talking cheerfully behind her. They even laughed once or twice, as though they were enjoying themselves. *Of course, they're enjoying themselves*, Megan thought bitterly. *Their ponies are behaving!* When Megan was able to glance behind her, she saw that both Zipper and Star now appeared calm and happy. They were walking along at a steady, flat-footed walk, their heads alert but relaxed. Ruth-Ann was waving her hands in the air, talking loudly, and Kendra was having a drink of water from her new purple canteen.

Megan couldn't raise her hands and wave them in the air. If she did, Blondie would probably jump as though Megan's hands were some sort of monster. Megan couldn't relax enough to have a drink of water. Instead she needed both hands to clutch wildly at the reins, trying to control her pony.

Megan hated the trail ride. For the moment, she even hated Blondie. All she wanted was to be back safe and sound at the horse trailer. And they had barely started the ride! It seemed as though they had been riding for hours, but when Megan did finally manage to peek at her wristwatch, she saw that it was only eleven!

They had been riding for only an hour, and it had seemed like forever. Blondie was still acting no better than she had at first. If anything, she was getting more and more agitated. The last time Megan had pulled back roughly on the reins, the little mare had almost reared into the air. She was now opening and closing her mouth, and her ears flicked angrily back and forth.

No, Megan and Blondie were not having a good time. Not a good time at all.

The Black Cowboy Hat

"We're almost at the corral," Mandy told the group.

Megan could hardly wait to get off Blondie. And she didn't know if she'd get back on or not after lunch. She didn't know what to do.

Megan glimpsed a family of five riding ahead of them. The father was riding a black horse and wearing a matching black cowboy hat. He had a medium-sized boy perched behind his saddle. The mother was on a tall chestnut horse, leading two small ponies, one on each side of her horse. Each pony had a young child seated casually on their backs, chatting happily.

Megan glared at the family.

That woman could ride her horse and lead two different ponies. Their horses were behaving perfectly, and they were all having fun. Megan couldn't ride even one pony without problems!

The family stopped their horses and moved over to the side of the road to allow the Ready to Ride group to pass. "Thank you," Mandy said with a wave of her hand.

Just then, an extra strong gust of wind came barreling through the trees. The father's black cowboy hat blew right off his head and across the road. Before Megan could do anything, the hat struck Blondie right on her rump!

Blondie went totally crazy. With one wild leap, she bounded forward. Her head went down, and her back feet shot up in the air as the little mare bucked once and then twice. The saddlebag bounced up and down on her back, spurring her on!

Megan didn't have a chance. She flew out of the saddle on the second buck and landed with a crash in a clump of rosebushes and silver willow.

Megan lay flat in the bushes and didn't move. Her face hurt where she had hit the rosebushes. Her ankle throbbed, and her wrist was sore. But even worse than the pain was the awful, embarrassed, angry feeling she had in her heart.

Her own little pony, Blondie, had bucked her off!

Blondie was acting horrible. Now she was loose on the trail, and for once Megan didn't even care what happened to her. *She can run away for all I care,* Megan thought. A tear worked its way down her cheek, and this time it was not caused by the wind.

Megan Finishes the Ride

When the group finally made it to the corral, they found Blondie securely tied to the wooden fence. The little mare seemed unhurt, but one of her leather reins was broken in half.

"I imagine she stepped on it," Mandy said.

"Good," Megan replied. She hoped that it had hurt.

Everyone was quiet as they sat down on the grass for lunch. Megan didn't feel like talking, and her friends didn't know what to say.

After they finished the simple meal, Ruth-Ann and Kendra walked over to the nearby outhouse. When they were gone, Mandy turned to Megan. "OK," she said. "What do you want to do?"

"I quit," Megan said. "I'm not riding Blondie anymore."

"You can do that," Mandy agreed. "But I've been talking to some of the grown-ups. They say that we can exchange horses, and you'll still earn your pledges for the Cancer Society."

"I don't care about my pledges," Megan said.

"Well, we can't just leave you behind," Mandy said. "You have to get back to the hall."

"I'll walk."

"If you walk, you don't earn your money," Mandy said. "Why don't you ride Seeker, and I'll ride Blondie?"

"You don't even know Blondie," Megan said, "and she isn't going to behave any better for you than for me!"

"Probably not," Mandy agreed. "But I am older and bigger."

"Why would God let this happen to me?" Megan suddenly exclaimed. "I was trying to do what He wanted when we entered the cancer ride. I thought He'd keep me safe."

"You're the one who knows about God, not me," Mandy said. "I never go to church."

"Today, I don't seem to know anything about horses or about God," Megan said unhappily.

Mandy thought for a moment. "Mr. Rawling said that sometimes God answers our prayers 'Yes' and sometimes He answers them 'No.' Maybe He isn't going to answer your prayer the way you want today."

"I guess not."

"Maybe God isn't real anyway," Mandy said. "None of my friends believe in Him."

Suddenly Megan felt a stab of shame. Yes, she was mad at Blondie. And she was confused about God for the moment too. But it would be awful if her feelings made her older sister stop believing in God.

"I want to be like Trish," Megan said softly. Then she thought for a moment and said it louder. "I want to be like Trish," she repeated.

"What do you mean?"

"When Trish told us about her cancer, she said that she had decided to trust God even when things didn't seem to be going very well. She said that God knows what's best even when we don't."

Mandy shrugged her shoulders.

"I'm going to finish the trail ride," Megan said.

"I could 'pony' Blondie," Mandy said. Megan knew that she meant she could ride Seeker and lead Blondie. "You could ride double behind me on Seeker."

"No," Megan said with a sigh. "That could make Seeker's legs sore. I'll ride Seeker, if you'll ride Blondie."

"It's a deal," Mandy said. She jumped to her feet. "Let's switch our saddles. And I want to longe Blondie for a few minutes and see if I can do something to get her to pay attention to me."

Megan watched as her older sister took all the girls' lead ropes and tied them together to make one long rope. She then snapped Blondie's bridle to the end of it and began to move the little mare around her in circles.

Blondie immediately began to buck. But this time, it didn't help her at all. Mandy just clicked her tongue and kept the mare moving faster than ever. When Blondie quit bucking, Mandy made her stop and switch directions and forced her into a lope again.

Within a few minutes, Blondie began to puff. Mandy didn't let her slow down. She forced the mare to stop, turn, and then lope off in the opposite direction. Every time Blondie began to fuss and pay attention to the nearby horses, Mandy just applied more pressure. Before long, Blondie began to look tired.

Blondie seemed somewhat calmer when the trail boss rode up to say the group was ready to leave. Mandy made a quick repair of the broken rein by using a lead rope in its place and swung into the saddle.

Megan climbed onto Seeker with a feeling of relief. The big Morgan mare was steady and calm underneath her. Megan rubbed her sore ankle and then gave the mare a squeeze to move forward.

Blondie was still goofy on the rest of the trail ride. Even with the bigger girl riding, the pony found ways to act up. She spooked several times at little things such as rocks at the edge of the road, and she squealed once and made a half-hearted attempt to buck.

But Mandy was able to keep the mare's head up.

Finally, they were back safely at the Hardisty Fair Grounds.

A Prize
for Megan

The girls spent quite a bit of time hauling buckets of water for the thirsty ponies and then hanging up nets full of hay. When the ponies were finally taken care of, they left them tied safely to the trailer and made their way into the crowded hall.

Megan went to the bathroom and looked at herself in the mirror. A long scratch went from top to bottom of one side of her face. Her hair was full of small pieces of brush and a streak of something—tears and dust, Megan guessed—ran beneath both eyes.

Megan washed her face and shook the twigs out of her hair. Then with a sigh, she returned to the tables for the barbecue supper.

After a big meal and two helpings of dessert, the girls settled back in their chairs. Megan's legs and arms were aching now, but she felt a bit of pleasure thinking of the upcoming awards. Blondie had been awful on the trail ride, but nothing could take away the fact that Megan had earned over six hundred dollars in donations!

Mr. Erickson, the trail boss, came to the front of the room and spoke into the microphone. He praised everyone for their hard work and dedication in helping to find a cure for cancer. "Two years ago I was diagnosed with cancer of the colon," he said. "Thanks to prompt treatment by my doctors, I was able to be here today to ride with you."

The crowd broke into a loud roar of applause.

When the room quieted, the man went on. "I'm here to tell you that cancer can be beaten. Forty years ago nearly every child that was diagnosed with leukemia died. Now we can save most of their lives! You *can* make a difference."

Then he began to award prizes for the different classes of riders.

The youngest-rider award went to a child hardly big enough to walk. "Jordan is two years old," the trail boss said. "And he rode the entire trip behind his father." A little boy and his father stepped forward to be presented with a brand-new saddle blanket.

The oldest rider was a seventy-nine-year-old man who took home a feed bucket full of horse treats as his award.

The rider who came from the farthest distance was a girl about Mandy's age. She had traveled from Washington State to ride with several friends. She explained that she was riding at Hardisty today to remember a local teacher who had died from cancer the year before.

Then it was time to award the prizes to those who had raised the largest donations.

The adult rider over the age of twenty with the highest donations was a woman who had earned more than three thousand dollars for cancer! Suddenly Megan wasn't so sure she was going to win a prize. Three thousand dollars was a lot more money than she had earned.

The youth between the ages of thirteen and twenty who had earned the most money was a tall boy who had raised almost sixteen hundred dollars.

And then it was time to award the prize for the rider who was twelve years old or under.

"And the winner is . . ." the trail boss announced, "Ruth-Ann Chow with nine hundred and seventy-six dollars!"

Ruth-Ann grinned and jumped to her feet. The announcer shook her hand and passed her a new red halter as her prize. "It will match my horse's saddle blanket," Ruth-Ann said. The crowd clapped again.

"I didn't know you earned that much money!" Megan hissed as Ruth-Ann sat down clutching the halter.

"You didn't ask," Ruth-Ann said.

Megan was happy for Ruth-Ann. But she couldn't help feeling a twinge of disappointment at the same time.

Today hadn't gone the way she had expected at all. Blondie had been a real brat. Megan had been bucked off for the first time in her life. And now she discovered that she hadn't won the prize for the highest donation either.

Yes, it was wonderful that the Cancer Trail Ride had earned so much money. That money could help people such as Trish. But the day would have been more fun if Megan had gotten something good out of the deal.

Just then a tall man with a black cowboy hat walked to the front of the room. He whispered something to the announcer, and the announcer nodded his head and whispered something back.

"I have one more prize to award today," the trail boss finally said, straightening back up. "The Rusk family would like to donate a prize called 'The Cowboy's Choice' award. This award goes to the person who showed the most bravery and perseverance during the ride. And today we would like to award this prize to— Miss Megan Lewis!"

The room erupted with loud applause and whistling. Megan blushed and then struggled to her feet.

The cowboy standing in front of her was the man whose black hat had blown off and hit Blondie! He shook Megan's hand and then handed her a piece of paper. On the paper was handwritten:

Please present this form to your local tack store, and we will pay for a free cowboy hat for you. You may choose any size and color that suits you best. We're very sorry for your accident, and we want to thank you for "cowboying up" when things got tough.

Bob and Julie Rusk

Megan was almost asleep as soon as they climbed into the cab of the truck. But as she closed her eyes, thoughts rushed through her head. *I need to talk to Trish and see how she's feeling. And I need her to give me some advice about Blondie.*

Blondie wasn't a bad horse. Oh, yes, she had been horrible today. But now Megan could see that Blondie wasn't ready for something as stressful as a crowded trail ride. Maybe she'd be different when she was as old as Seeker. But maybe not. Even so, there were many things that Blondie did very well. Trish couldn't teach riding lessons this month. But surely she could give a Ready to Ride girl some advice.

And I need to talk to Mandy, too, Megan thought with one last sigh. *I want her to see that God's perfect, even when people like me aren't. Maybe I can make a difference in Mandy's life too. Because God certainly makes a big difference in my life. Even when things don't go the way I want.*

Words of Advice About Safety With Ponies

Is riding a horse dangerous?

If you ride a quiet, well-trained horse or pony and if you are supervised by an experienced adult, then horse riding is no more risky than most other sports. But there are safety rules in every sport, and riding is no exception.

Several years ago, I was nearly hurt in a horse accident by a pair of very quiet, well-broken, trustworthy horses. Why? Because I made a mistake. My daughter, Kaitlin, and I tied our horses to an older hitching post. My Paint horse's lead rope was just a wee bit too long, and he was able to reach down and nibble on some long grass. When he went to raise his head, the rope caught behind his ears. My horse panicked and pulled back, frightening my daughter's horse which had been standing quietly beside him.

Both horses pulled back with all their strength. They were tied to the top post of the old hitching rail, and it pulled lose from the side rails. Now both horses were still tied to the top post, but it swung free between them. The post had several long spikes fastened to the ends, and as it pulled free the nails stabbed both horses in the chest.

It could have been a disaster. Horses can run wildly when they're frightened and hurt themselves by running through a fence or even knock a person down. Luckily, these horses only took a few steps and then stopped. Because they were normally quiet and sensible, I was able to free them from the post without anyone becoming injured.

Was the accident my horses' fault? No, I made a mistake. Actually, I made two mistakes—first tying my horse too loose so he could get caught in the rope, and second, by tying them to something that wasn't strong enough to take their pull.

Here are a few other horse-safety rules when working your horse from the ground.

1. Always wear boots to protect your toes when working around your horse.

2. Do not run, yell, or move quickly near your horse. There are two types of animals in this world—predators and prey. Some examples of predators are lions, cougars, wolves, dogs, cats, and people. All the members of this group have eyes in the front of their heads. They all hunt—or could hunt—prey animals. Examples of prey animals are mice, deer, cows, sheep, rabbits, and horses. All these animals have eyes on the sides of their heads so they can watch for danger. They need to be alert so something doesn't come along and eat them! Normally, they escape predators by jumping and running away from danger, but if they are trapped, they will fight back. Never forget that the biggest horse is really no different than a timid mouse. When he's frightened, he may try to run away or struggle to protect himself.

3. Horses have blind spots under their heads and straight behind them. Try to not approach

your horse from these spots as they will not be able to see who you are.

4. At first, lead your horse from his left side. This is how most horses are trained to obey. With time, you can teach your horse to lead while you are on his right side, but it takes practice.

5. *Never, ever,* wrap the lead rope or reins around your hands, arm, or waist! Sometimes people have been worried they wouldn't be able to hang on to their horse, so they tied the rope to themselves. Then when the horse panicked they were dragged behind the running animal.

6. Tie a horse to strong, secure objects only. This means you can't tie a horse to wheelbarrows, truck mirrors, or boards on a fence. Tie a horse high enough that he can't get a leg over the rope. And use a quick-release knot so you can free him quickly in an emergency.

7. Never duck under your horse's neck when he is tied. You will be in his blind spot, and if he were to pull backward he could easily strike you with his front hooves.

8. When you walk behind your horse, stay very close to him and speak quietly so he knows

you're there. If your horse were to kick when you are nearby, you would be pushed more than actually kicked. If you are a few feet behind him when he kicks, you will be hit with great impact and could be seriously injured.

9. Always keep yourself in a safe position when your horse is tied. For example, do not stand in a narrow space between your horse and a fence. If something frightens your horse, it would be difficult for you to escape.

Don't let these safety rules frighten you away from the wonderful sport of horse riding. I have ridden horses all my life, and I have never been seriously injured. (OK, I've had a few bruised toes and even a sprained ankle, but that's all!) And all sports have a dangerous element—whether it's hockey, skiing, or motorcycling. You just need to follow the rules and you'll limit the chance of being hurt.

I hope God blesses you when you ride. And I hope you are a blessing to your horse and to the others around you too.

Happy trails,
Heather Grovet

Love Horses?

Just for You! From Pacific Press®

Coming Soon! Ready to Ride Series Book #6

Super Star Problems (Ages 6–9)

Kendra has worked hard to prepare her pony, Star, for the upcoming gymkhana. But on the evening of the races her new next-door neighbors set off fireworks, and frighten the ponies. Star is injured and can't compete at the gymkhana. Kendra is disappointed and thinks the other girls are unkind because they are still excited about being in the show.

Paperback, 96 pages.   ISBN 13: 978-0-8163-2255-8
ISBN 10: 0-8163-2255-4

Ready to Ride Series (Ages 9–12)
Set of books one through three

(Book 1) **A Perfect Star.** Kendra, Ruth-Ann, and Megan form the Ready to Ride (R2R) Club and begin taking riding lessons.

(Book 2) **Zippitty Do Dah.** Ruth-Ann and her friends give pony rides to kids to raise money for an orphanage. They asked God to keep all the riders safe. So why didn't God answer their prayer?

(Book 3) **Good As Gold.** The girls participate in a real horse show, competing against each other. No one could've predicted what would happen and what the girls would learn from it.

Paperbacks. 4333003844. (**Sold in sets only**.)

Order from:

1 Local Adventist Book Center®
2 Call 1-800-765-6955
3 Shop AdventistBookCenter.com